Unearthing Inner Gold

Tristen Vieaux

ISBN:

DEDICATION

THIS BOOK IS DEDICATED TO ALL THE COURAGEOUS ONES WHO DARE TO FEEL THEIR FEELINGS, LISTEN TO THEIR HEARTS, AND EMBRACE THE BEAUTY OF EVERY SEASON.

CONTENTS

INTRODUCTION

I wrote initially to comfort and express what I was witnessing and experiencing. As I watched the world I had once known shape and contort into something different, the process of self-expression through poetry encouraged, soothed, and ignited a passion project that became a constant companion over these multifaceted past few years.

Complex and constant, a woman's heart is layered and ever-changing. Much like the various conditions nature places on display through its seasons, the terrain is rich with beauty, movement, and depth. Come share with me in this soulful journey of introspection, rebirth, growth and gratitude through the transformation of every season.

The poetry of *Unearthing Inner Gold* illuminates my complex journey of finding love and self-compassion in every season.

Through life's seasonal transformations, I journey to unearth what it means to be a woman, embrace love, compassion, and keep an unwavering faith in God while navigating the struggles of being a human.

MY STORY

My story has many pages
A creation of moments in time
Chapters filled with
Tears and joy
Inspiration and defeat
Disclosures and vulnerabilities
Depicting
Choices made
Sacrifices and heartache

Chapters filled with
Travels with roadmaps
Wandering on roads unknown

My story
Beautifully unfolds
Blank pages yet to come

Winter

"Introspection"

Though my soul may set in darkness, it will rise in perfect light.

I have loved the stars too profoundly to be fearful of the night.

—An Astronomer's Prayer

365

Opportunities to embrace my inner joy
To love myself fully
Like fast moving frames
Snap shots of time
Artful moments that live within
1 second
1 minute
1 hour
1 day
1 week
1 month

A gallery of events contained within
60 seconds
60 minutes
24 hours
1 day
4 weeks
12 months
Opportunities to love myself fully
A masterful gallery of snap shots housed in the container of
365 moments in time

Lovely Soulful One

You are beginning a journey
You are
Embodied courage

For every self-doubt
You find a way to persevere
Pushing through the chaos of this world

Like a raw gem
Your potential and beauty is endless

You remain steady in the storm
Rooting down
You find deeper meaning within

While the future of today may feel unknown

You ARE
Strength
Graceful
Contagious

You ARE lit from within

Like velvet covered steel
You are beauty and strength

As every season brings
Change
Uncertainty
Challenge and
Growth

While in days you may feel weary
You are
Never faint of heart

You overcome and transform
Yet true to who you are becoming

You are grounded
yet
Soar

Pages

Words on a page
Chapters in a book
Each feeling turns into a word on a page
Each thought creates a paragraph
Each decision morphs into a chapter

Multiple choices culminate into themes of my text

What is the culmination of my pages

Fantasy
Adventure
Romance
Mystery

Every moment
Thought and choice imprints upon the pages of my book

May my pages
Illustrate
Illuminate
Inspire

Wishes

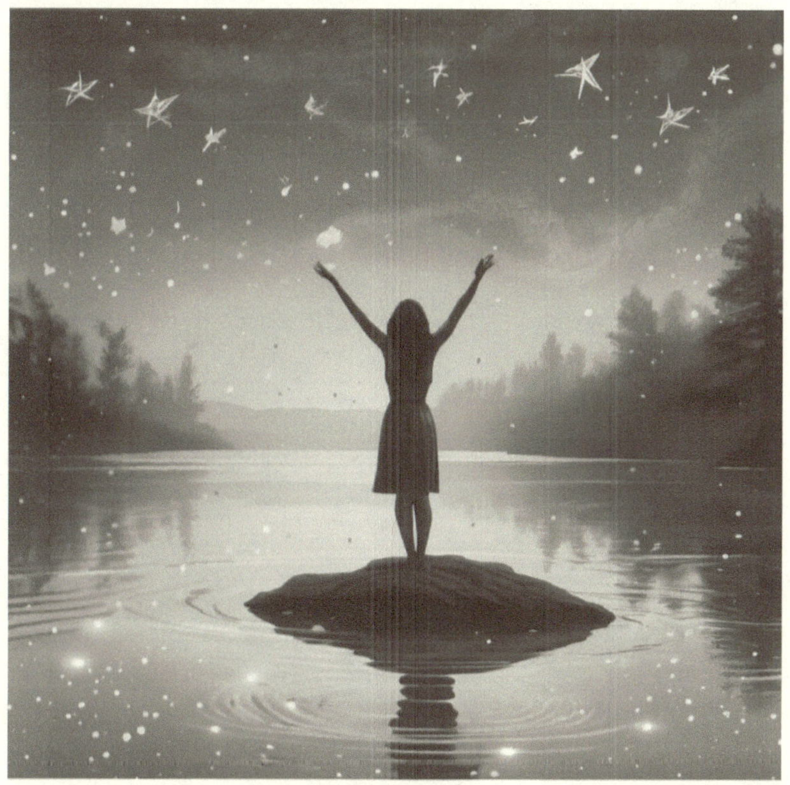

Skipping rocks across the water
Casting glances on falling stars
Throwing pennies in fountains
Holding my breath just to blow out candles

Could these wishes be a
Mirage
A tormentor of what could be

And yet....
Maybe...

Never arriving?

Phantom wishes
Something created from a fairy tale

Fairy tales have one believe that a woman needs to be rescued

Let it be known

These wishes are not of a woman who needs to be saved!

These wishes are a creation earthed out of a courage to experience greatness

Passionate
Powerful
Mind blowing
Spine tingling
Life changing

Moments that simply
Take your breath away

Be bold
Take heart, dear one
Close your eyes
Inhale
and
Make a Wish

Refiner's Fire

Hot embers ignite
Destruction
Renewal
Passion
Change
Transformation

Scorched earth- creation and health
Burned bridges- changes in heart
Fiery inferno- Transforms an Old creation awakened renewed
Refiners Fire-Alchemist treasure revealed

In Fire, burning is put in motion
A creation
Beauty unearthed

Rest

Rest is a mystical being
She asks for little, simply stillness
Her gift is everything we ever need
Rest
Comfort my being
l invite to sit in the throw blankets of my heart

Heart Condition

When my heart is heavy
I miss you
I miss me with you
I miss the possibilities that my heart conjures

Feeling the things I cannot change
Noticing the desires that do not serve
Feeling the draw always and never

I want
Passion

    Felt presence
Connection
  Fire
Depth

My heart feels
heavy
Floating
sinking
Burdened
  unhinged

Always and Never

My heart beats with knowing
The fire is ever present

Your voice ignites

Your eyes enlighten
Your words extinguish

My hope slowly sinks
My heart feels heavy

Noise

Noise in my head
Thoughts speed like a bullet train
Emotions cycle on repeat
Longing
Confusion
Hope

Eyes focus and unfocused
Searching for
Answers
Solutions
Missing pieces

The thoughts get louder
The emotions stronger

Noisy with a desire to find meaning
Clumsy with self-doubt
A fast-moving train
Destination unknown

Noise….
Where is the volume button to my heart?

Breath in
Breath out
Be still

Breathe in

Breathe out
I pause

Broken Melody

My heart skipped a beat
Lost the note

There is a vacancy
The kind of dark tar like space that brings forth longing

Memories and desire stick to the frayed edges

Mind replaying incomplete images of fractured moments
Like a needle to vinyl
Stuck in this groove of a scratched melody

Once beautiful

Now a tormenting tune
On repeat
Never moving forward

A musical cadence
The end of a melody
Lyrical lethargy

Awaiting new notes

My heart skips within this vinyl illusion

A new melody never plays

The needle is held captive within its deep groove

My heart sinks
As the
Needle skips and

Repeats

Snowflakes

Snowflakes fall from a frosty grey sky
Crystal gems that dance and sparkle
Frosty falling clusters of white and shimmering silver
Culminations of intricately cut icy glass

Form glittering mounds of delicate ice
Land upon my cheeks

Each snowflake more beautiful than the last
Each create a frozen wonderland made up of intricate art pieces

Brief and joyful crystalline moments

Pause….
Inhale
Take in her beauty

For once eyes looks away
The moment has past
That unique snowflake that landed in all her silvery splendor

Has melted and returned to a
frosty grey sky
To return as something new but never the same

Wine

Your sweetness greets me
Your robust stature
Your earthy essence beautifies
Clouds my thoughts
Blankets my heart with warmth
Enhances my senses
Emboldens my desires
You are the instigator of passion
You argue with my better judgment

Much like a woman who knows her value
With age you improve
And are
Beautifully complex

Pieces

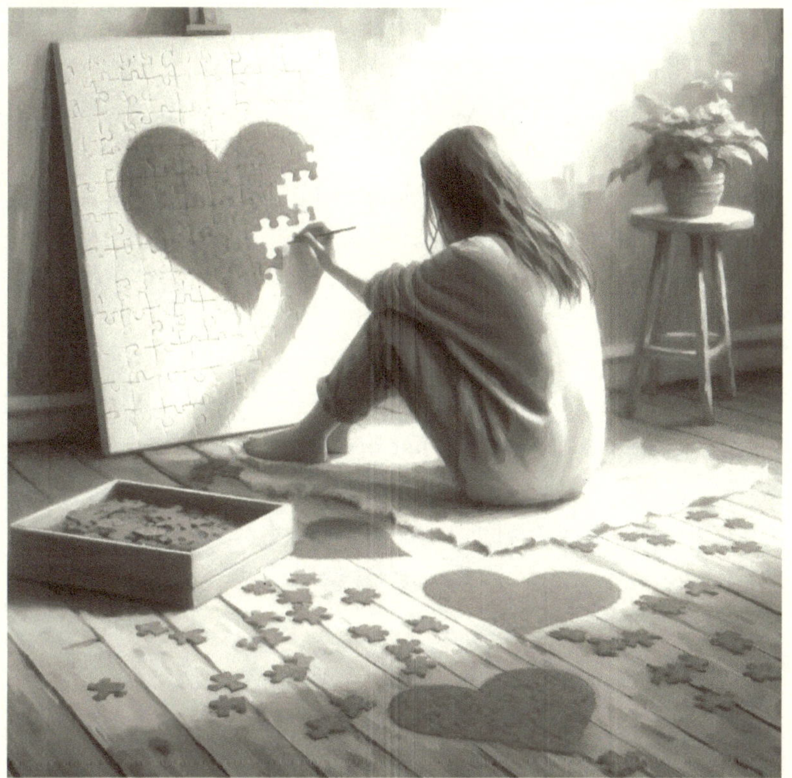

Collecting the pieces of my heart
Glimpses of beauty
Fragments of light
Reflect back
Courage
Boldness

A fiery strength to love
Adoring perseverance
I carry the truth of all things
I hold dear

Disappointment

Disappointment is
A manifestation of a different outcome than what was hoped for
An attachment to a desired result of being
An opportunity to open up windows
Let the light in
To shine in a new way
Envisioned space for a different outcome
A place to exhale concrete expectations
Limiting internal messages that no longer exist
and
Breathe into the life that is yet to be seen

Quiet

You are my

Solace
Keeper of secrets
Observer to thoughts
Comforter
One who calms
Generous listener

Strengthener to my soul

Windows

Some say that the eyes are the window to the soul
What if mine are bloodshot and fatigued?
Revealing hours of crying
Tears of pain
Fear

Unknown and flooded with questions of past
Countless decisions

All a culmination
Of "what now "and " how much more ?"

What if my soul is so much more than the pain represented in my eyes
More than those that depict a sleepless night?

Windows can be
Smudged
Foggy
Frosty
AND
Beautiful portals to light

Windows come in all sizes and conditions

Make no mistake
While my eyes are weary
Never underestimate the strength of this soul

Longing

Heartfelt ache
I reach for your hand
You pull it away
Expression of love
No connection
Only silence

Spoken words
Free fall into nothingness

Your emotions are like
A no vacancy sign
Lackluster like burned out neon

Blank
Void
Cold

Longing for something
Lost between us

Something that was
Or
Maybe never there

The longing of another
A representation
A mirror image

All that is good in me
A reflection of my beauty upon the stillness of a midnight lake

Moonlight castes shadows
Magnificent and magnetic

Longing has found meaning
She has found home within me

Fear

The goal is not to suppress her
She is wisdom
Listen and observe
Lean into her fury

Notice how....
Always stay....

What form does she take and to what purpose does she serve?
Dictator
Coach
Protector
Teacher
Friend

As a dictator she presents as
A larger-than-life booming voice that shouts insults and shames me to believe
I am not enough
Good girls don't do that
You are worthless
You CAN'T do that!

Fear is sometimes a coach that whispers
"Not yet"
"Wait"
"It's not quite your time"
As a Protector

She presents with the
Ferocity of a lion baring jagged, sharp jaws
She roars, growls and keeps me safe

While as a teacher
Fear prompts me to traverse across gravity defying
suspension bridges stretched high above the trees

She encourages me to believe I am stronger than I think I am

Friend and fellow adventurer
I take her hand and trust that her parachute will open as I
take a leap from my securely buckled airplane seat into a
bottomless bank of clouds

Fear is all these things

BUT
She will never be my captor

Tender

Intentionally I unfurl my clenched fists of control

Craving deeply
Growing
Making contact

Feelings glow like fiery embers
Exposed

Vulnerable to the elements

My inner most thoughts
On display

My Insecurities
Flash like molten coals

My skin
Feels inside out
Exposed nerve endings

My soul bare

Tenderly
I relinquish falsehoods of self

I lay myself open
I am raw

I breathe deeply
I let go

Sadness

A
Flicker
A
Spark
An Inner Fire

A perceived and felt pain that something can no longer be as it is
A choice to
Feel and be moved
Be curious
Be ignited

Embracing the transformation
No longer
Ignoring
Smothering
Extinguishing

The sadness is proof of God within
Bearing witness to the experience of all that is human and broken

Sadness is
The candle that shines into the dark corners
Presenting a knowing of all that has been and yet to come

Messy

Feeling the feels
Images arise

Feeling messy
Feeling the mess

My heart is clouded
My mind swirls

Dust storms of uncertainty
Profound grief
Heavy sadness encapsulates me like woolen blankets on a hot summer's day
I gasp for breath
My soul yearns to break free
From all that is messy and cluttered within

There is also joy
An unseen yet palpable
Hope

Embedded in this mess

There is another realm
Moments that embody

Vibrant paint splatters onto a blank canvas
Plumes of powdered sugar from a flurry of baking

Strewn linens that lay across my bed lazily after a blissful
afternoon nap

Each messy moment of this cluttered and chaotic life
Present a gift

This mess called life turn each into a
Beautiful and cherished
And yet

Profound
Message to be held

Locks

To whom behold the keys
What is locked for protection
What is off limits
What is closed for a season
What is locked for a lifetime

What is mine to experience
What is not mine for the taking

Who decides
Who holds wisdom

Desire
Envy
Pride
Drive
Need
Surrender

Which of these do I consult/ embrace

Is it I who has always held the keys?

Locks

Which one will I choose to open and for what purpose does it serve?
Gift

Challenge
Tempter
Potential
Love

I am the holder of the keys
My fate, wisdom and gift

I will choose with intention what key to open my own

Locks

Heartbreak

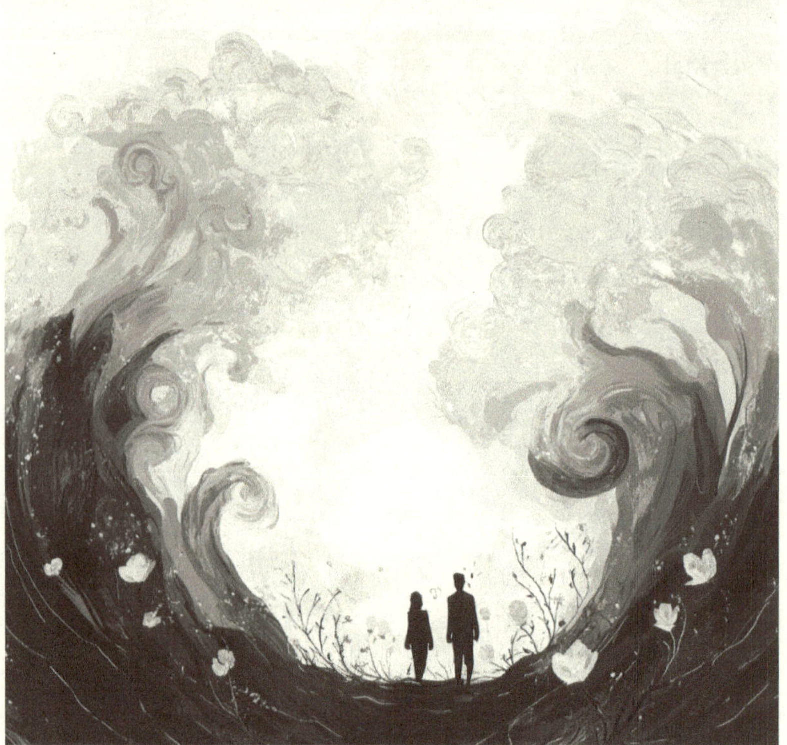

Electric sadness

Love or Projection?
Both melt to a felt sense
A connection of two souls

Heartache
The truest felt sense of humanity
Masterful wave
Collision of pain and spirit

Heartbreak
A Teacher
An ever-present reminder of boldness and grasping

A courageous pursuit towards an unknown outcome
Heartbreak
Electric sadness
May my soul heal
May I
Risk to love another day
Rise above the chaos of spirit and soul
Embrace pain with
A courage to heal

Silence

In the silence
I ponder

I worry
I angst
I conspire
I dream

May my silence inspire
Healing
Creation
Introspection
Wisdom

Peace

Shadows and Light

Shadows grow and shrink with light
Shadows dance and move
Shadows follow my lead

Embracing the dark with the light
Intertwined with rays of sunshine and moonlight

I dance within the shadows and the light
I embrace all aspects of this shadow
As this Shadow is
My Shadow
One that reveals all that is divinely and uniquely mine

In the Shadows

In the shadows
I find a place to hide
A place of comfort

My soul aches to be known

Yet- the scars of past bonds are tender
A reminder of what once was
I retreat back into the familiar dark corridors
A place of refuge

My heart beats with hope
Yet- The broken off pieces lay scattered at my feet
A feeling of pain surges
Memories of risks and things left unsaid

My eyes catch a sparkle in the mosaic of glass at my feet
A light shines

Illuminating the ground beneath me
Something awakens my senses

Pulling at the hem of my skirt
Light is my shadow's companion

My shadow does not exist without her
Dancing
Beaming
Glittering

I look down at the pieces and see beauty
The stories unfold and transform the initial pain, heartbreak and fear

Stories that reveal themes of
Alchemy
Refiner's Fire
Abundance and
Growth

I embrace her
I step out of her shadowy refuge into the light
I stand in boldness and take my companion's hand

I am comforted in her magnificent light
I thank my shadow for her protection

We walk hand in hand with intention
We dance and move with light

Contemplation

I am still
My heart beats
My eyes shift upward in reverence
The heavens open
My heart expands
Grounded yet light
My soul contemplates over well-worn paths
Roads yet to be traveled
Moving adventures
Yet in this moment
I am still

I pause to listen to my heart
Attunement
Light
Contentment

In the quiet I find
Solace
Joy
Peaceful pastures
I am embraced in her loving grace

Waiting

My heart
Waits in a room without windows
Spaces without light
Only darkness
Wandering around
Bumping into the spaces of words yet to be uttered
Answers are withheld or mysteriously unknown

A beautiful view of what is and could be
Held within the life corners of my mind's eye

Hope
Inner light is revealed

Soul felt recognition
I sit still in a room without windows, now peaceful

I see beauty unfold within
I no longer wait in darkness
I am the light
Answers I seek reside within me

This dark windowless room lacks nothing
I am free to explore, embrace and love

I no longer wait for light for the light is within me

The windows appear within this dark room
I am released

"Spring" Rebirth

The beautiful spring came, and when nature resumes her loveliness, the human soul is apt to revive also.

- Harriet Ann Jacobs

Spring

An annual promise
Dynamic and ever changing
Presence of frost
Painting branches
Sunshine then brings warmth
Melting of protective layers
My heart stills
Finding hope
A new beginning
She prompts earth to shift
Encourages renewal
Scattering seeds
My soul grounds
Life springs forth
I breathe in

Hope

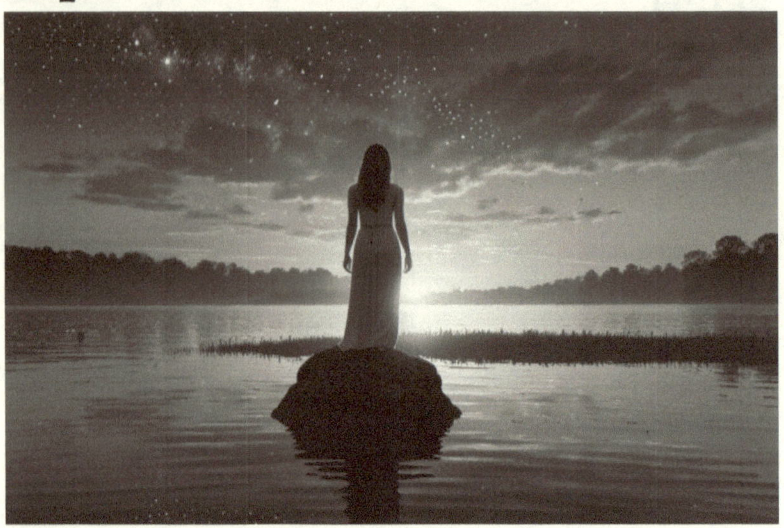

Hope moves me like
Dancing beams of light
Stars sparkling in a black onyx sky

Ripples on water
Intentions like waves

Moods fluctuate
Impulses rise

Dreams inspire movement
Fire ignites change

Alchemy of the soul

Sunrise
Transformative

Nurturing
Curative
Hope invites me in

Enchantment

She is the glitter in a moment
The beauty experienced in a smile
The way moonlight dances on midnight

The caressing of waves of water upon the sandy shore

The promise of sunrise each morning

Pause
Observe
Breathe in

Be confident in knowing
For every moment
will present enchantment
For she is you

Weatherproof

I am Weatherproof
Snow showers
Rain drops
Strong winds and lightning storms

Not today

I have enough on my mind and too many things to do

Prepared for whatever the day brings
I won't let the uncertainty of storms hamper my joy

I have my rubber boots so that
I may dance in the rain
My hat and mittens to conjure up a mysterious snowman
A sturdy striped kite to soar high amongst the winds and storms

Nothing can dampen my plans for today

I am prepared
I move boldly into the unknowns of today

For I am
Weatherproof

My Body

My body is a
a landscape of
Strength and beauty
There are Seasons of tranquility and turmoil
A place where
My mind can feel like a treacherous terrain,
Rocky and Harsh

At times

My lungs can feel hollow
While others
My heart swells with life
Encouraging my legs to keep moving
My hands to keep grasping for
What is inherently mine

Life
Movement
Love
Compassion

Oxygenated cells
Uniquely make up

This body
My companion
Friend and
Cherished space

Time

Moments of time
Like light filtered through tangled branches
A lonely leaf that collects
droplets of rain

While
Time
Moves and dances
Nourishes and edifies

She cannot be
Collected
Stilled or
Paused

She
Calls
Commands and Prompts

Attention
Reverence
Immediacy

Time is a

Philosopher
Teacher
Traveler

She is
Steady
Stealthy
and

Never fails
To touch
Stretch
and
Move

She is a constellation of stars across an ombre sky

A Splash and ripple
She moves oceans waves with her breath

She prompts the rotation of moon and sun across the skies

Time
Has many faces in which she appears

Those who experience her want to contain her and yet she is profoundly

Missed
Desired
Wished for
And
Anticipated

Always fleeting

Paper Thin

I am fragile and strong
At times my skin feels as if inside out

I
Perceive
Feel
and
Experience
All
Deeply

My skin is paper thin
She tries to protect
In the guise of an armored heart

Paper thin beauty
Stretched across a delicate and sturdy landscape

A fiery soul
Emotions filtered through a kaleidoscope of colors
Feelings surface like a
Rainbow of colors on a painter's pallet
A multitude of paint brushes
Saturated
Ready to create
Paralyzed at times with a multitude of images
Jumping off the page of my imagination

I am all things embodied in color, sound, touch, imagery
I am
Strength and Paper thin

Love

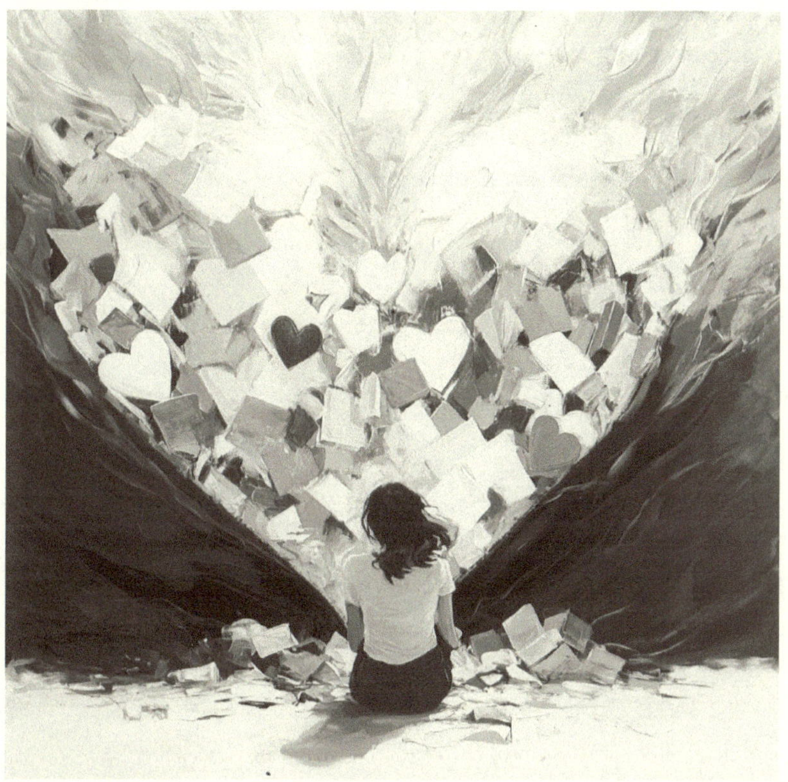

Whispers to me
Awakens my senses
Knocks gently to enter my heart space

I open the door
You enter my tidy space

You takc off your shoes
You scatter your things all over the floor
You turn my world upside down

Chaotic
Frenziedly
All consuming

When you, my love, enter
All that I have known is changed
Forever
My love
I am changed

Tears

May these tears water the seeds of my soul

Tears of hope
Tears of joy
Tears of sorrow
Tears of anger
Tears of renewal

May there be healing
May there be inspiration
May there be redemption
May there be reconciliation

Breathe in Darling

Breathing in dark
Exhaling light

Shaking off the weight of my humanity
Shedding layers of my own insecurities

Tapestry of soulful color
Building new layers
Interwoven threads of spirit
A delicate mis match of beauty, tears, joy and felt presence

Breathe in darling
You are fire

Learning to Dance in the Rain

Honor your inner child's wisdom
She knows life is not to be taken too seriously
She prompts us to
Jump in puddles
Laugh in the face of conformity

Act like every moment is an adventure
Embrace the mud

Embrace the storm through the eyes that
Anything is
And
Can be possible today

So I
Dance in the rain

Paper Flowers

Painful progression towards hope
A stride forward

Ahhh… how exhilarating

Temporary moments
Hope turns to uncertainty

Did I dream this healing or is this a reminder of my present
pain in the working out of my shadows

I observe my humanity in humility
I love myself gently in this painful transformation

I am a work in progress

I am fiery and complex
Who loves largely
Who feels things immensely

A warrior woman wrapped in paper flowers

Rise

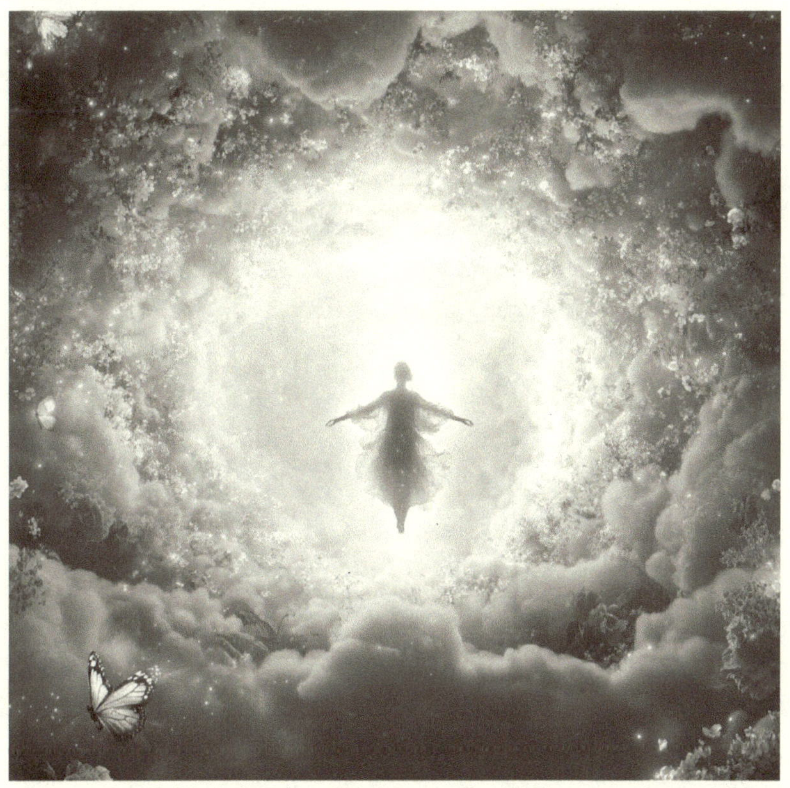

Darling
Believe and know you are perfectly created

Rise above what is
And
Embrace all that is lovely within

Birth Rite

Life cycles
Taking our first breath
We inhale and exhale
A loud cry
Our first moment of self-expression
We find our voice naturally
We take our first steps

We
Stumble
Fall and get back up naturally
As time moves forward
The world tells us

To be quiet
To sit still
To make room and share with others
We learn to make ourselves
Small
Polite
Agreeable
All in the name of
Being liked
Fitting in

We silence and question what at one time came naturally
We trade in our birthright
To see our inner wisdom as
Other

Wrong
Selfish
Lazy

We contort and squeeze our spirits into what we believe are socially accepted
We are bound to a cage that was never meant for us

We seek outside the bars of the cage
Longing
Aching

Aspiring to
Break free
Be loud
Breathe in greedily
Take in as much of this beautiful world
We claim our birthright as it presented so naturally at the start of this messy, exposed life

We
TAKE UP SPACE

We
breathe and exhale

We
lift our voice to the very heavens whence we came

Joyfully
Exuberantly
Freely

Claiming what is ours!

Doorways

Doorways beckon, invite me in

Clear glass doors that shine wide open
Solid wooden doors that obscure views to what may be

Doorways
One radiates golden light
Promise

Hope

Another glows with mystery

Unknown paths
Conscious and
Unconscious decisions

Doorways that connect:
Soul
Heart
Spirit
Bliss
Joy

With intention and boldness
I swing open the door
I embrace the invitation of my
Doorway

Paradox of Perfection

In my mind you are perfect
A balance of complexity and ease
A reflection of my contradictions and a companion for catharsis
Emotionally connected and self-aware
Regulated AND passionate
Energetic and calm
Beauty and grit
Adventurous and stable

A picture of all things I strive for and desire

The perfect mix of yin and yang
Sunshine and rain
Sweet and spicy

You meet me in the places of my
Concrete expectations
A room filled with
Black and white curtains
Rusty and outdated control levers

You pull back the curtains revealing shades of grey and light
I loosen the grips of my perception
And question

All that once was perfection
Staring at the broken levers that once kept me

Controlled
Safe

And
Scream loudly
Messily

I am Liberated
Free from all that was once perceived as needed

The myth that perfection ever existed
And
Savor all that is beautifully imperfect and
Mine

Obsession

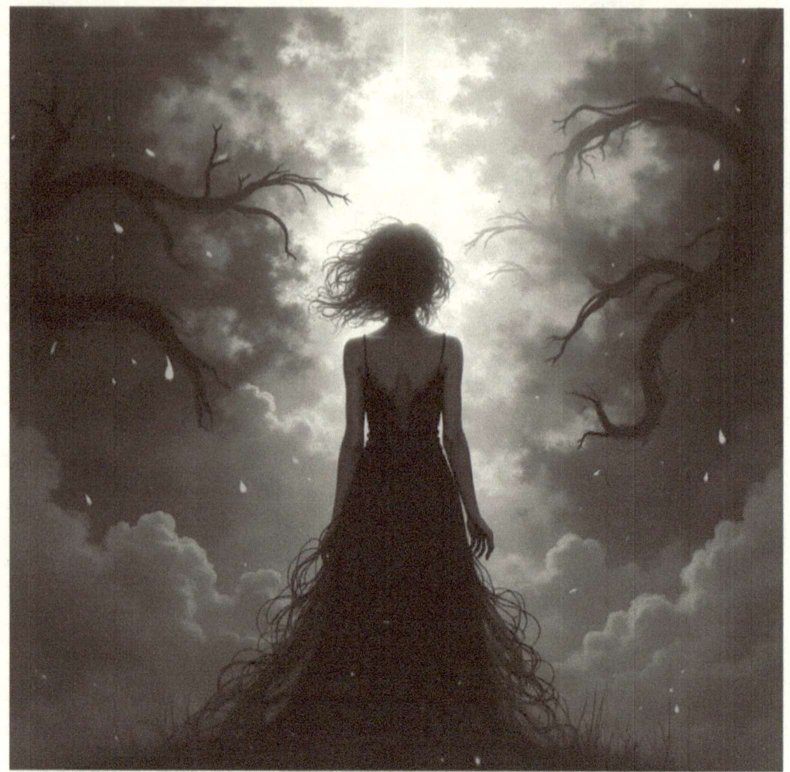

You are always with me
Sometimes more present than others

I feel you
I deny you
I am a mixture of delight and burden

I find you in all things

My love takes shape with the passing hours of the day
The memories encapsulate a moment

Microseconds can change perception
Senses adjust to the ardent feels of this second

I reorient and find meaning within

I discover myself transcendent
I float above needing you
I embrace my strength inside
The outer workings of me
I am
Soulful
Shiny
and
A glorious independent being
I am Free

Anxiously Aware

My emotions spiral
My limbs feel heavy
Deep felt weight of what is yet to be

I am in this world and yet not of it

In moments
A traveler through time - sturdy and prepared

A fairy sprite-who sparkles and is carefree

In my anxiety
An alien who doesn't know the language or how to make contact

In awareness
I navigate and float
I am earth bound AND sublime

My anxiety manufactures
Unknown paths
Steamer trunks filled with
Ripped maps

Potholes and
Missing road signs

My ancestors whisper from beyond
I feel their grip
Expectations for more

I stand in my personal journey
Awareness that speaks, encourages and loves the unknowns

I am a spiral of anxious awareness that I am all these things
I am prepared
I sparkle
I am earth bound AND sublime

Anxiously Aware
I am all these things

Awakening

Today my heart awakens
to the gentle melody of promise in possibilities

Much like the forest awakens to the whispering winds
amongst its tall trees

An ocean surface awakens to the movement of waves and
ocean mist

A desert landscape warms amongst the ripple of sunlight

Awakenings are in the subtleties of moments

May you embrace my spirit
May your gentle presence reveal within me my possibilities

Daring to Bloom

My fiery soulful one
A seed that dares to be born into earth
One that follows her destiny
Fear never stunts her potential
Promise only propels her forward towards growth

She
Floats
Enchants
She risks and buds
She embodies courage
She is beautiful
She embraces her potential

Overcomes adversity and
Blossoms

Summer

"Growth"

In the midst of winter, I found there was, within me, an invincible summer.

- Albert Camus

Felt Sense

I feel the warmth in your presence
Growing within depth of every breath
I find you in unexpected moments
Inspiration runs deep
Like fire Igniting
My soul is connected to something I can't see yet I know is there

Sparks of
Joy
A flutter of heartfelt light

My being dances with anticipation
Awaiting
For When
We embrace

She is magnetic
She is me

Lightning

Lightning lights up the distance
A crack of thunder
Jolted consciousness

What once seemed far away

In my peripheral view

Now commands attention
Sends tingles
Electric curiosity
Oh how a storm stirs….

Wonder
Fear
Excitement
Anticipation

When will the next electric shock shatter the black night sky?

How many seconds pass before the next crash of thunder
shatters the silence?

Smells of damp earth
Sounds of the patter of rain on fallen leaves

What once was autumn
Hibernation of mind

Ignites
Electric night

Now
Awakens my soul's being from the grip of my summer-like slumber

Just Because

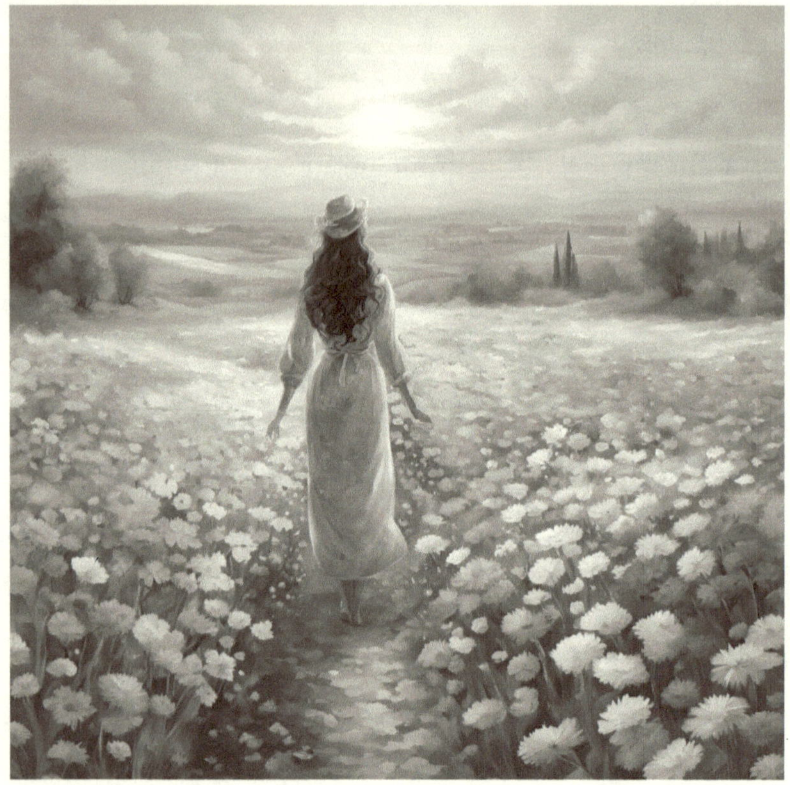

Flowers
Colorful and fragrant
A special blossom to mark every occasion

Bulbs nestled tenderly among the aroma of rich soil after a soft rainfall

Seeds scattered amongst dark rich earth

Blooms that are gathered

Bouquets assembled

The most beautiful flowers of all are the ones collected

Just because

Garden Full of Lilacs

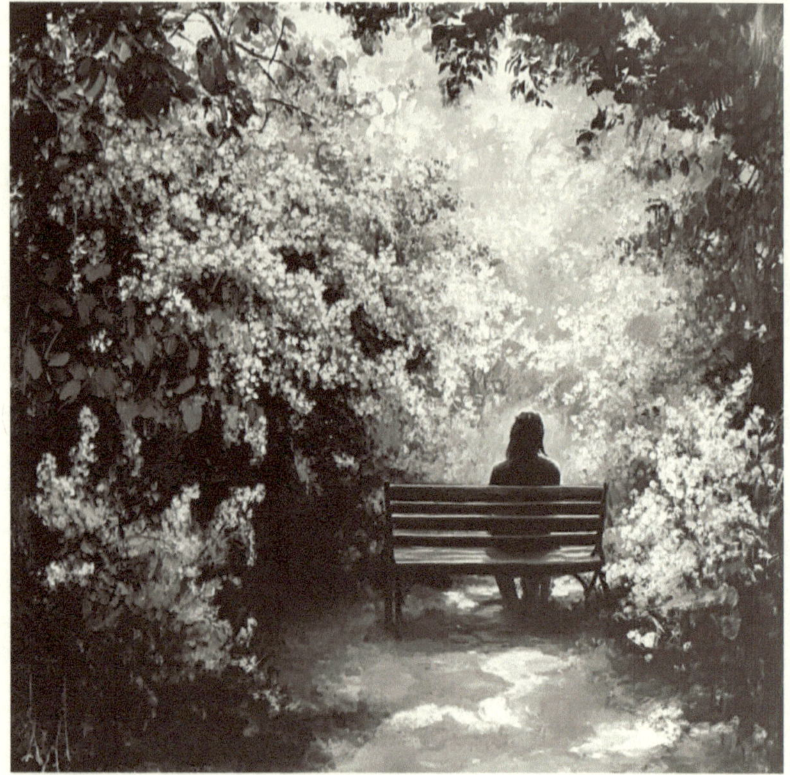

In a garden full of lilacs
You meet me here
Trembling
Vulnerable
Sparkling
Sitting on a weathered rustic bench
Lush branches provide shelter full of deep purple and white blossoms

My soul dreams
As I breathe in this

Fragrant
Intoxicating moment

intertwined
spirits
visions
Heart beats

Deeply aware of
The allure of
Past and present
Various versions of self-shared within the many spring times of light and shadows

This beautiful lilac garden
Where my soul awakens, ignites and feels deeply

I am brought back to you

Transformation

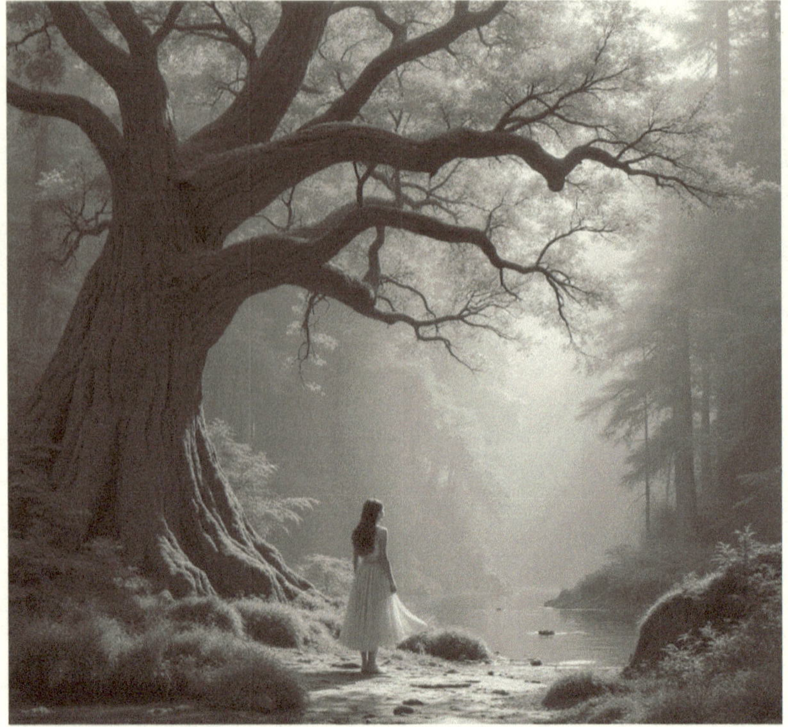

Nature embodies and reminds us that transformation is possible

Through nature a gentle prompting occurs
Encouraging us that the way towards a new beginning
Exists within

Like the rings of a tree
Our bodies are historians
Etched in earthen vessels
Deeply rooted images of
All things past and present

Freedom

Flowers on my wall
Hide the cracks
Conceal the holes
Camouflage the water-stained facade
Presence of past storms are concealed

Hope stirs
Colorful and vibrant

New growth
Tiny flower buds
Blossom within the crevices
Taking root in the in between

Flowers splash painted petals onto this crumbling wall

Transfixed
Rays of sunlight illuminate an opening

My gaze falls onto a green weathered wooden gate
A gentle wind brings movement
A mockingbird lands upon its surface

Sparks renewal
The gate creaks open
I am transported
I am free

Forest Bathing

Bathing under the shelter of your branches
Earthy and peaceful
I deeply Inhale you
You embrace my senses
Beholden lover

One who holds me and quells my anxieties
Calming, peaceful and always present

You
Comfort
Nurture
Breathe life and
Resuscitate my soul

Rain

Rain
Giver of life
Nourishing
Cleansing

Quencher of drought
Nurturer of cracked earth

Rain Fall
Renews grimy pavement like a baptism revealing new landscapes

Rain
Awakens my senses
Refreshes my soul

Your presence brings bows of light through the dark clouds
Rays of color through the mist

Rain dances and sways
Moving
Undulating

Creator of moody melodies
Bringer of transformation to each passing season

Lovely Darling

A life lived is
Never forgetting the awe
Embracing the unknowns
Loving yourself in all seasons
Surrendering to joy
Dancing limbs a flailing
Singing no matter- just sing
Jumping to follow your heart- even if…
You are afraid

Take the trip
Be late to the meeting to linger a little longer in joy

Bask in the Art of Nothing and Everything

A life lived is the one you love, reach for and embrace fully….
Loving yourself in every season

Lovely Darling, You ARE the Life

Fun

You are an idea and a twinkle
A whimsy
A tingle
A red balloon set loose upon the backdrop of a blue sky
Rising into the clouds
Smells of coconut sunscreen and salty air
Sounds of laughter and splashing waves

You are my companion who invigorates my inner child
A Music maker
An Invoker of joy

Fun is the
Animator to my limbs
Toe tapping feet
Dancing under a canopy of possibilities

The promise of a new adventure

Folding clothes and preparations
Suitcases filled with old train tickets and remnants of
seashells

Dreams of
Beach walks
Falling into the surf
Playfully laughing
Lingering moments
Hoping to find a way to pause the clock

Still time

All that is desired is
In this moment
Your hand in mine
Intertwined hearts

Salt on skin
Wind swept
Riding this wave of emotions

Bursting at the seams of these suitcases as the sun melts into hazy purple and orange horizon of this moment

We have now

Presence

Swaying back and forth
Like the limbs of a tree
Rooted and steady in the grounded earth
The dance of indecision moves with an audience of sky and clouds
Emotions change like colors fade upon the horizon at sunset
I am a tapestry of indecision, color and movement
I am
Bold
Dynamic
Fragile
Uncertain
Beautiful
Joyous

Here- present

Spectrums of Light

Bring me to my fullest self
Streams of light
Illuminate dark corners
Twilight
Stirs familiar longings
Sunlight
Inspires hope and determination
Moonlight
Seduces, invokes dancing and soulfulness
Life spectrums of
    Vibrancy
    Dimming
    Illuminating
    Failing
    Spectacular feminine light

Sky Full of Stars

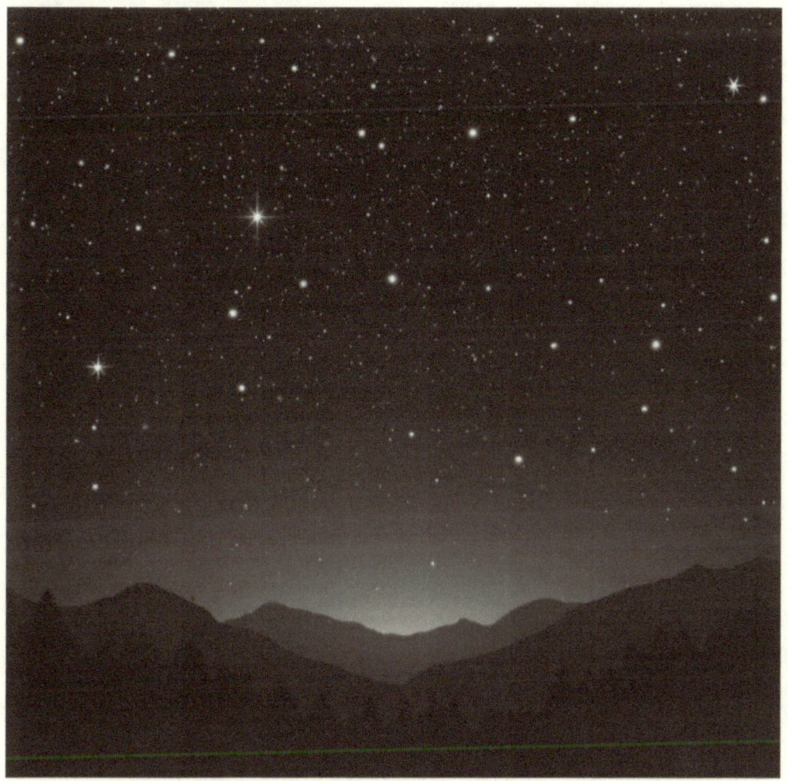

A sky full of stars
A layered landscape of color
Willows and Wildflowers

I embrace the many shades of this desert

The whistling of the wind through the brush
The sound of wild horses in the distance

Vintage airstreams under dancing meteor showers
Once lost, artful souls connect
Dreaming
Wandering
Discovering

This lost soul has discovered the artful beauty of
This layered landscape

Wildly I cherish
Wildly I love
Wildly I will dream under
A sky full of stars

Tide Pools

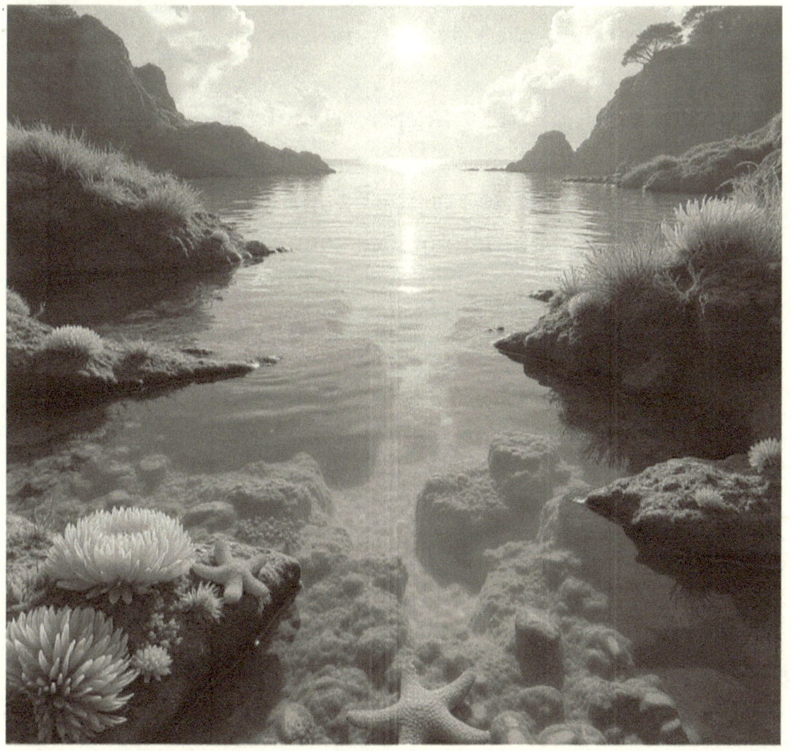

Tide pools
Fractals of light ripple
Reflections of clouds dance

Sunbeams penetrate like golden rods through the liquid turquoise surface

Some are shallow
Others run deep

Life and abundance live within these tide pools

Anemones for protection
Starfish for divine love and inspiration
Abalone symbolize the power of these oceans' waters

These tide pools are full of depth and meaning

A joyful dance of life and depth
My heart longs for the abundance within these waters

My soul is suspended
within these life giving tide pools

Deep Blue

My deepest blue

Are found in the depths of this ocean
Bodies of water that move in layers of turquoise, cobalt and sapphire tones

Shades of blue have imprinted my soul

The blue that paints the skies at dawn and brushes the heavens at dusk

Blue is the color of desire and hope
Adventure and life represented in these multi-tonal shades

Blue is the color of my love
Represented in the
Soulful waters of my heart
A world full of oceans and seas

Where my breath is paused
My pulse rises
My mind is free to float in the vastness

My desires are reunited to her dreamer

My soul catches her breath
She exhales in the promise and beauty

Deep Blue

Where my heart and soul are intertwined
My passion and refuge unite

Staring at the Sun

Brilliancy
Intensely felt
Encapsulates my heart space
Heavy and pure
Dense and luminous
Penetrating my being
Like looking at the sun
The power is dangerous, overwhelming, and potent
Internally consuming and desirous

Like a tidal wave
Precious and powerful

Like staring at the sun

Starling

Sings a melody
Breaking the silence

Wings that soar
Splashes of color

A cage with an opening
A place to rest
Never a captor
Always free

Inspiration

Inspiration, like a
Traveling songbird
I awaken to your distant melody
The movement of leaves rustle underneath my window
You call

The movement of your wings
Wind carries and lifts your voice
Through the eaves of this house
Through these open windows I find solace
A portal that connects me to you

I find you in the in between places
In the stillness you are present
Like wildfire
My soul is awakened
Creative sparks ignite

My traveling and inspirational songbird
Love guides me to you

Pebbles

Pebbles upon the seashore
Layers of sand move underneath my feet
The rustling sound of seagulls wings as they soar high above the rocky cliffs
Jagged limestone peaks rise high out of the waters to caress clouds
This coast is made up of pebbles
Each stone tells a story
Represents a moment in time
One no more important or less significant than the other
A reminder no matter how small
Everything makes a difference
In the landscape of this beautiful life

Lessons

Learning to communicate my needs, desires and intention
with
Clarity
Compassion

Music lessons
Attuning to the beat of my own heart
Playing polyphonic notes of felt emotion
with
Grace
Fluidity

Dance lessons
Learning to sway and move my body to what my soul reveals
Belly moves
Limbs flow
Embodied joyful movement

Life lessons
Teach me
    To speak peace, love and encouragement
    To listen with understanding and loving intention
    To BE authentically Me

Containers

Place holders to put lost things
Vessels that at times are chipped and cracked

Placed on shelves and bookcases
Missing lids
Fallen and shattered to pieces

Containers
Forgotten
Misplaced

Beautiful and flawed containers

Inside
Treasures discovered
Missing puzzle pieces found
Photographs
Postcards
and
Letters portray
The beating hearts of past and present lovers
The joy of family get together and long lost friends

Containers filled with
Road maps to places once been
Picture books of desired faraway places

Paper clips and thumbtacks
All reside within my containers

Vessels that hold both light and dark
Beauty and pain

Unearthed potential
Ready to be discovered

Beauty

Beauty like love is in the eye of the beholder

Elusive
Painful
Fleeting

Beauty of
Nature
Spirit
Teaching
Perspective

Beauty is a
Companion
Captor

Like a thief in the night
Comforts like a sweet sultry melody
Captivates like rays of gold and purple light across a twilight sky

Beauty moves like
Sunset at dusk
Burning comets scattered in the cosmos
Falling rust colored leaves upon damp earth

Beauty
My ever dynamic, fickle and vain companion
Rise to greet me today

Fall-
"Harvesting Gratitude"

Let me rejoice in the harvest of each day. Transform me into a song of gratitude. Enfold me in the circle of your Time-Enduring-Now.

—Macrina Wiederkehr

Gratitude

In a world full of
Maybes
And
Some days

I am glad there is now

Family Table

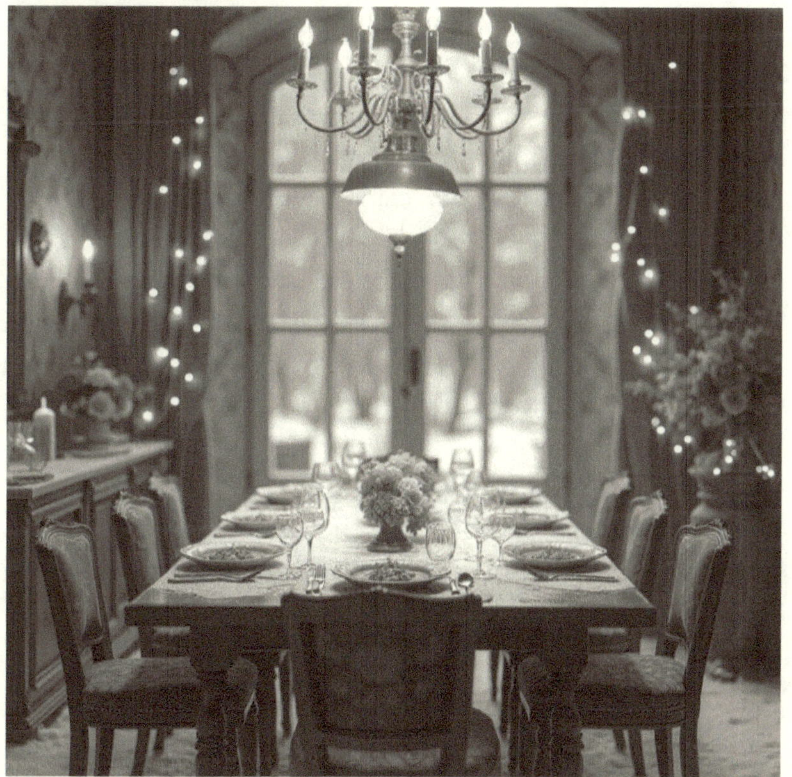

The ritual of a family meal
Lovingly planned
I pour over cherished recipes
I tenderly collect ingredients

A splash of this
A dash of that

Hands rush to prepare a love letter filled with the bounty
from a cupboard

My heart skips with anticipation as I smell the aromas that
greet me from the oven and bubbling stove pots

The table has been set

The dishes carefully prepared
Each holding a soul felt appreciation and tenderness

Each dish emanates warmth embraces and envelopes

Cherished and well loved

We kick off our shoes
We settle into the comfort of an array of colorful cushions
Where we experience nourishment and grace
Shared connection over casseroles and conversations

An essential pause to punctuate the end of a day

Each loving member gathers
Settles in

And

Exhales….Gratitude
This moment
This ritual

For this
Family table

Home

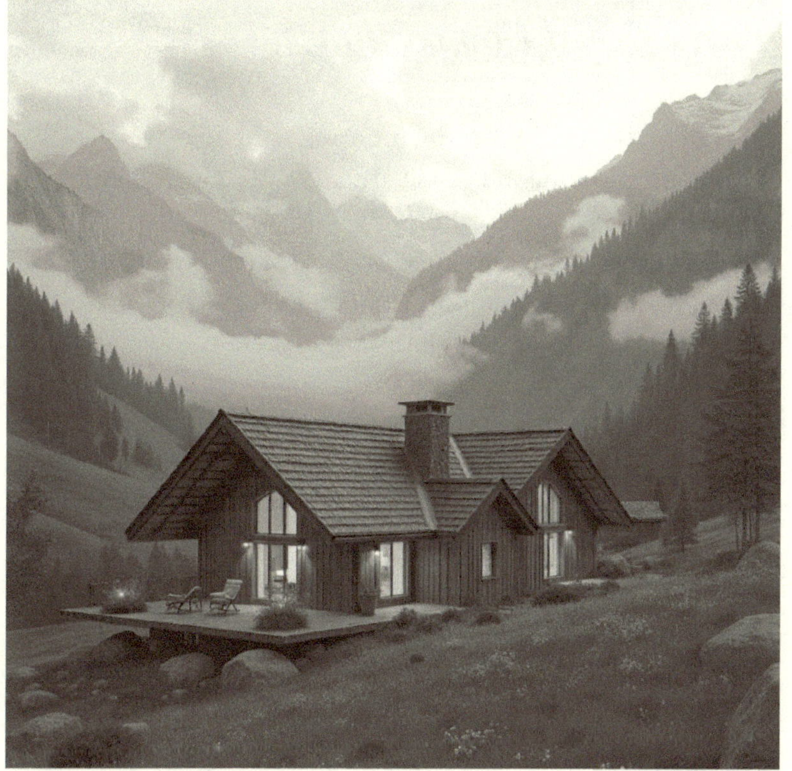

Home is
A steamy cup of coffee
A fluffy blanket
The smell of baked bread
Fresh warm chocolate chip cookies from the oven
The sound of a crackling fire

Feeling the expansion of my heart with every deep breath of gratitude

Knowing my value

Furry Loyal Companions

The ones who greet us in the morning light
Showering with unconditional affection no matter what
Those eyes that look up adoringly
The way those same eyes close lazily to say " I trust you"
Through family celebrations, skinned knees
Heart breaks and jumps of jubilation

Our companions are compassionate and ever present
Always there ready to rejoice with a wag of a tail or
Curl up next to us to lick away tears

Steady
Loving
Always present

Our companions are a
Reminder
Reflection
Unconditional love embodied in
One faithful
Furry being

Circle of Fire

An orange and yellow glow in the distance
Sparks of hot embers light up an inky dark sky

Mesmerizing, captivating, drawn in

Circle of Fire
Ignites promise, passion and life

Honoring
Elemental Fire
Metamorphosis
Transformative

Circle of Fire
Unchecked, Consuming, Powerful

Greedy
Out of Balance
Dangerous
Destructive

Circle of Fire
Reverent
Humble
Graceful being

I hold you with gratitude and reverence
Giver of

Elemental change
Illuminator
Teacher

Salvation

Salvation is the evidence of things hoped for
A free gift not earned
The power of true love
Transformative and eternal
Saving Grace
Embodied Truth
A place to rest one's anxieties
Perfectionists need not apply

In salvation we are accepted
Alchemy from steely human hearts to
Golden vessels of beauty and hope

In salvation we are
Loved
Forever changed

Pathways

Intertwined and tangled
Desired Roads upended
Crooked lines and hairpin turns
Heartfelt adrenaline

Where does your pathway begin and mine end?

My soul adventure has blurred into you
Where does mine begin?

The pathway that seemingly connected two souls

A needed detour
Now a closed exit ramp

I detach and detangle my
adventurous and yet weary limbs from yours

I embark with renewed passion for all that may reveal

My loving sojourner
May you rediscover your torch
to your
Heart Felt illumination

Shelter

My soul longs for Shelter

In the chill of early morning
I dream under a patch work quilt of my own thoughts

In the heat of midday
Fragrant orange blossoms lull me to breathe in and pause

In the sunset of dusk
Golden threads of light
Illuminate all that is possible

In the evening
Layered blankets of mystical stars invite me to rest in wonder

Moments of
Layered tattered tapestries
Woven gnarled limbs of ancient Methuselah trees
Mosaics of fallen peddles and leaves

I am safe to explore my inner being

I Shelter in these soulful places

Searching

Searching
Pauses between
So many unknowns

What is in these spaces?
Projection of the golden love within

Ignite the passion from unfelt
depths

Knowledge of my truest self-reflected back to me
Nothing within the eyes that look back at me
A searching outward
And yet vacancy

Spaces in between
Discovered aspects of self
Joy
Meaning
Purpose

Awareness that the joy within was never in those eyes

Everything and nothing existed
Held between two people and an intense gaze

Searching and yet
Nothing
I shift my intention away from you

You were never meant for me

My heart goes inward
I return my gaze to my truest self
Soulful, welcoming, compassionate
I breathe deeply, a sigh of relief
I am home

Letter to Those Who Wander

Letter to those who wander
The one who finds joy in the simple:
The sound of the rush of water over jagged rocks in a stream
The call of a the distant melody of a lone birds morning song
The sensation of a cool autumn chill upon skin
The golden reflection of sunrise that illuminate the dark
shadows of night
Those who wander and find joy in the simple
May you pause and notice the blessings that abide within you

Tapestry

I am a tapestry
A Unique woven beauty
A life illustration of Intricate colorful threads

Some made of wool and twine
Some threads stained and frayed
Others shine in gold and silver light

My life experiences on display within this artwork

A Wonderful and painstaking creation

A tapestry interwoven within a lifetime
My experiences on display show My
Pain
Love
Heartbreak
Struggles
Scars
    and
Beautiful artwork of choices

A lifetime of experiences on beautiful and humble display

I am strong woven beauty

Phases of the Moon

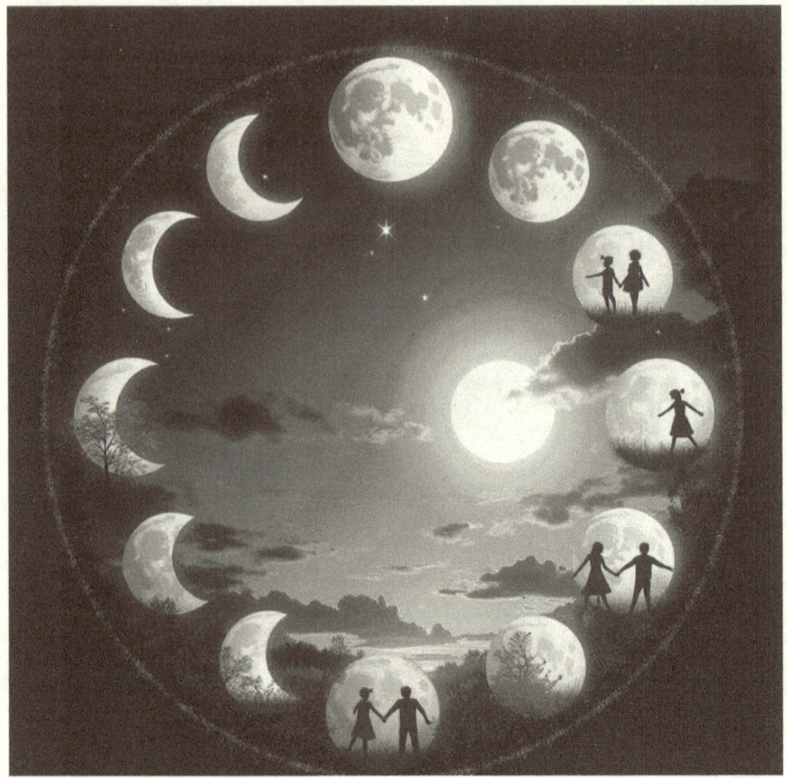

Much like the phases of the moon
Such are the many phases on one's existence
Tentative and wobbly first steps
First day of school
Lost front teeth
Crooked smiles
Finding one's way on the playground
Skinned knees and release of training wheels

First kisses and awkward dances
Broken hearts and new loves made

School plays and talent discoveries
Driver's license and fender benders

Self-exploration and testing wings
Found passions and graduations

Self-inquiry and self-doubt
Love lost and love renewed
Life moves forward
Like the many phases of the moon

Promises made and commitments entered like roots of a tree
One begins anew

Careers, family, a home is made
Celebrations of life and dreams are construed

Life ebbs and flows like the phases of the moon

Evaluation and determination
Grit and gold
Self-inquiry and transformations are made

A life manifests, breaths and moves

Like the many phases of the moon

Falling

Instantly Lifted up to the heavens
Sensations within float and electrify
In a flash
slammed back to earth
Crashing
Holding on for dear life
Parallel
Universes

Reality is within the eye of the beholder
Promises made
Even if just to myself

I am the holder of my heart
I create the fire
I ground the live wire of my soul

I am not the creator of my chaos
I repeat to myself as I experience
This falling over my better judgement

Swirling, heart pounding, crashing back down to

face myself

Falling….

Caffeine a Love Story

I await your morning appearance with loving anticipation
Your aroma awakens me from my dreamy state
Your morning presence excites my senses

Your steamy warmth illicit tingles
Your strong constitution is boldness in a cup

I drink you in

Friendship

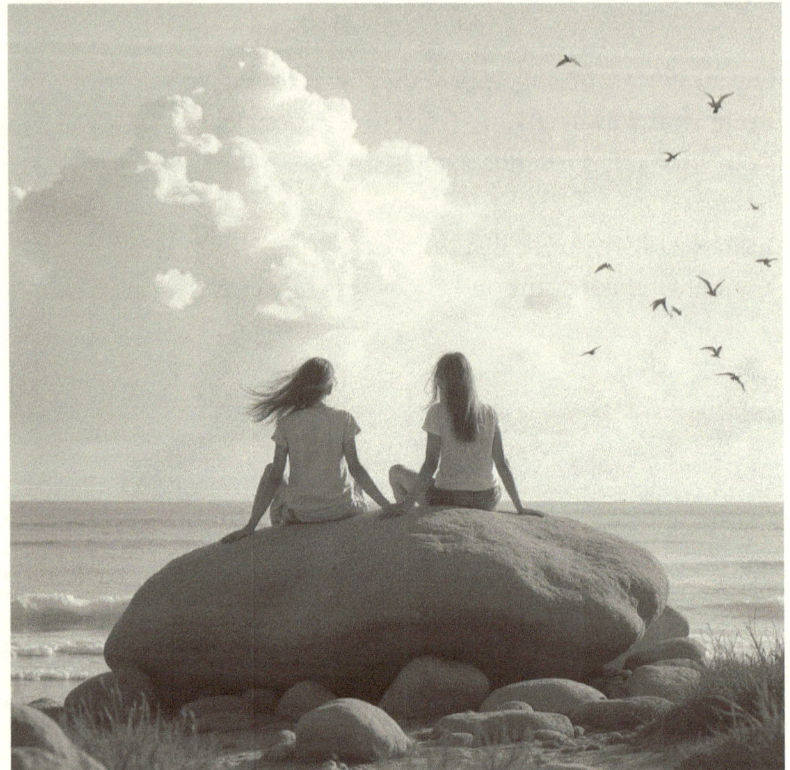

You are a rock
A needed light
Illuminating

You are the reassurance and encouragement after a long day
A kind presence that always brings laughter
Never lets me take myself or life too seriously
A constant companion to navigate the unexpected pitfalls
My soul adventurer
The traveler to help traverse the landscape of this crazy uncharted life

The one who lets me be me

You reflect to me the beauty of what I treasure most
You are the best part of me

Possibilities

Creator of dreams
Giver of whimsical wings to wavering spirits

Hope springs forth
She Embodies softness and strength
Golden light flows from her fingertips
A Tender and constant presence
Bringing forth vulnerability
Whispering promises of things yet seen
Waves of grace encourage compassion and peace
She is eternal
She propels all things forward
A muse for all things possible

Seasons

Seasons of
Grief
Joy
Transformation
Renewal

Falling into love
Out of love
Back in love

With one's self,
Outside of one's self
And
Finding that love was always there within

Owning our story and loving ourselves through that process is the bravest thing that we'll ever do.

-Brene Brown

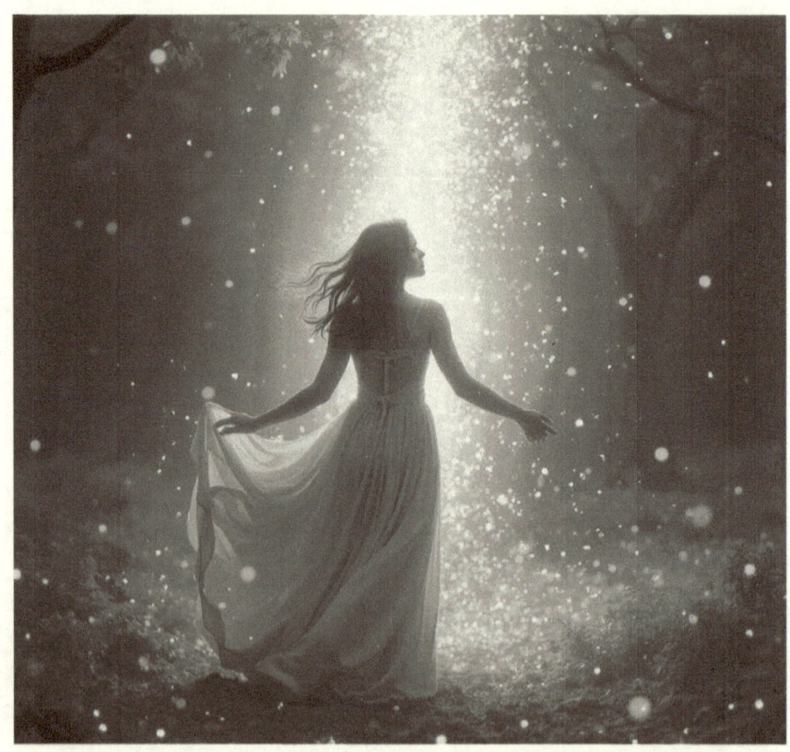

www.ingramcontent.com/pod-product-compliance
Lightning Source LLC
LaVergne TN
LVHW051007080826
845145LV00009B/2504

* 9 7 8 1 9 6 5 8 6 6 4 7 4 *